It was a beautiful day and Mikko, the little hedgehog, was
feeling completely content. He lay in his garden, watching the
clouds. As they changed shape, they reminded him of certain
animals or plants.

Mikko loved his garden. He knew every flower, all the herbs,
and even all the weeds by name. More than just their names,
though, Mikko knew about all their healing powers.

The little hedgehog also knew all the animals who lived there:
the reptiles, the mammals, the amphibians, even the insects.
Above all, he knew the birds, by sight and by their songs.

Suddenly, a voice shattered his thoughts. "Ha, look at you, lounging about in the garden, dreaming the day away, you lazy good-for-nothing!" It was Grandfather Tarek, who was out for his morning walk.

"The youth of today are simply useless," said Tarek. "When I was a boy, it wouldn't have occurred to me to sit around all day long, staring into space. You should *do* something!"

"But Grandfather, I *am* doing something," answered Mikko. "I'm watching the clouds, and observing the plants, and—"

"Ridiculous. That's absurd—wasting your time, squatting in the grass, sniffing the flowers! You should take advantage of your youth to accomplish something important so you will be happy!"

Mikko answered, "But I'm quite happy here in my—"

"Impossible! Go and take a look how others lead their lives!" Shaking his head, Grandfather limped away.

Mikko was confused. He didn't think that Grandfather Tarek looked particularly happy. What did others do that was so much better? the little hedgehog wondered. I will have to go and see for myself. Perhaps I'll learn something from them. He tied up a knapsack and headed off.

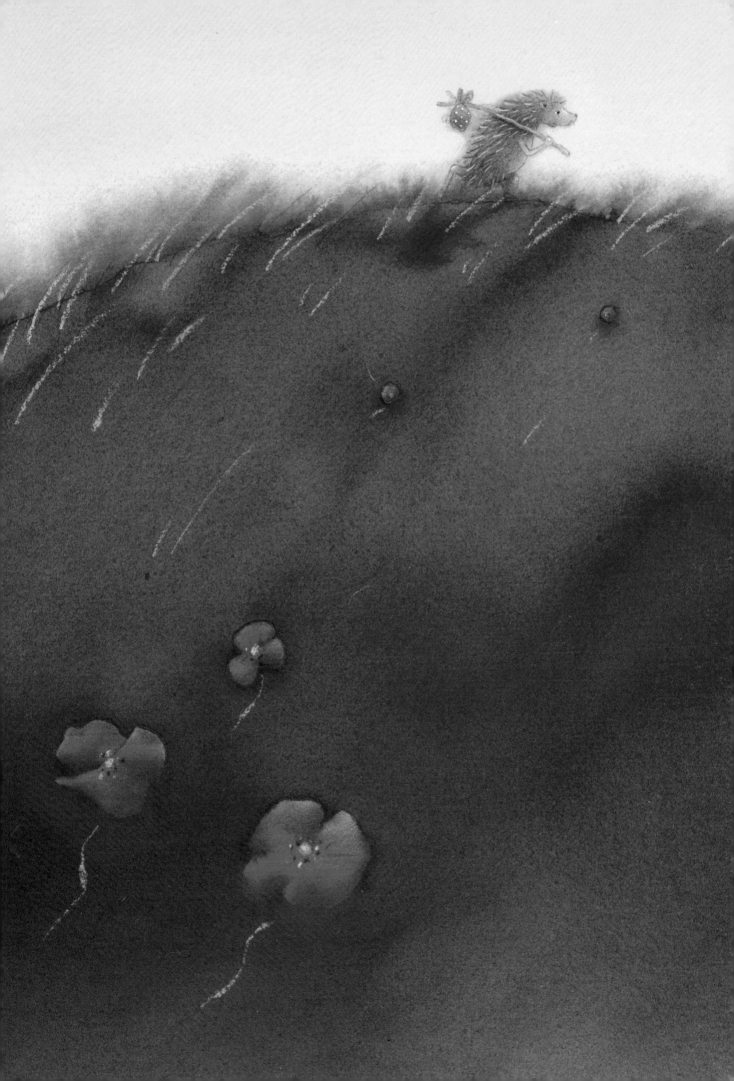

Suddenly, a tortoise sped by Mikko.

"Hey, Tortoise, wait a minute!" called Mikko. "Why are you running?"

"I'm in training," she panted.

"Training for what?" asked the little hedgehog.

"Training to be the fastest tortoise in the world."

Mikko scratched his forehead. "Isn't it a bit difficult to run with such a heavy shell on your back?"

"Of course it is," said the tortoise. "That's why I have to keep on training! But if I become the fastest tortoise in the world, I will be famous and happy!"

That sounded good to Mikko. "Let me run with you," he said. And so the two took off.

But Mikko soon gave up. He was completely worn out. The tortoise just kept on running; she didn't even look back.

Oh, dear, thought Mikko. Running can be fun, but not like this. He rested for a moment, then continued on his way at a slower pace.

Suddenly, a hare hurried across his path.

"Hare, wait! Are you also in training?"

The hare looked baffled. Mikko noticed the notebooks Hare was carrying.

"Training? No, I'm going to school."

"To school? What's that?" Mikko asked.

"Come along with me," Hare answered, "and see for yourself."

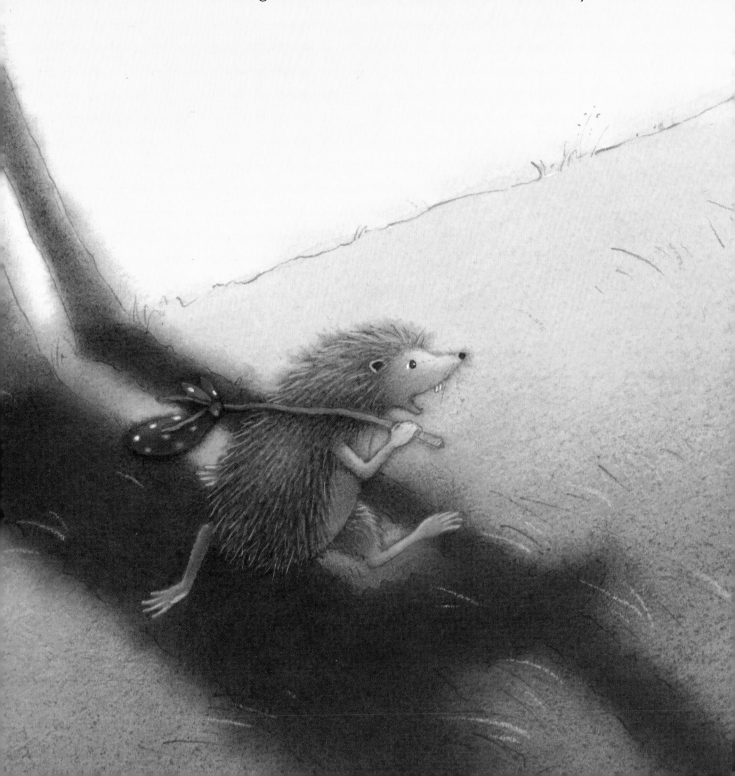

"All right," said Mikko, and followed the hare to school. Mikko hid behind a tree and watched. The teacher taught addition, subtraction, geography, and penmanship. Mikko couldn't understand a word. During playtime, he found Hare.

"Did you understand all those things that the teacher was talking about?"

"Are you kidding? I understood absolutely nothing," the hare answered. "I just memorize everything. My head will be so full when I have finished. Maybe one day I will be the most brilliant hare of all, and then I will certainly be happy."

The hare said good-bye and hopped back to his seat in school.

Mikko slipped away. He thought, You know, it is great fun to learn new things, but just memorizing without really understanding them is not what I want.

Deep in the woods he heard a terrible grunting and growling. In a small clearing, Badger was trying to lift up a gigantic stone.

"Can I help you?" Mikko asked.

With a terrifying roar, the badger heaved the stone high over his head, and then suddenly let it thud to the ground.

Mikko jumped back. "You almost flattened me! What are you trying to do?"

"I'm building up my muscles. I want to become the strongest badger in the world!"

Oh, no, not again, thought Mikko.

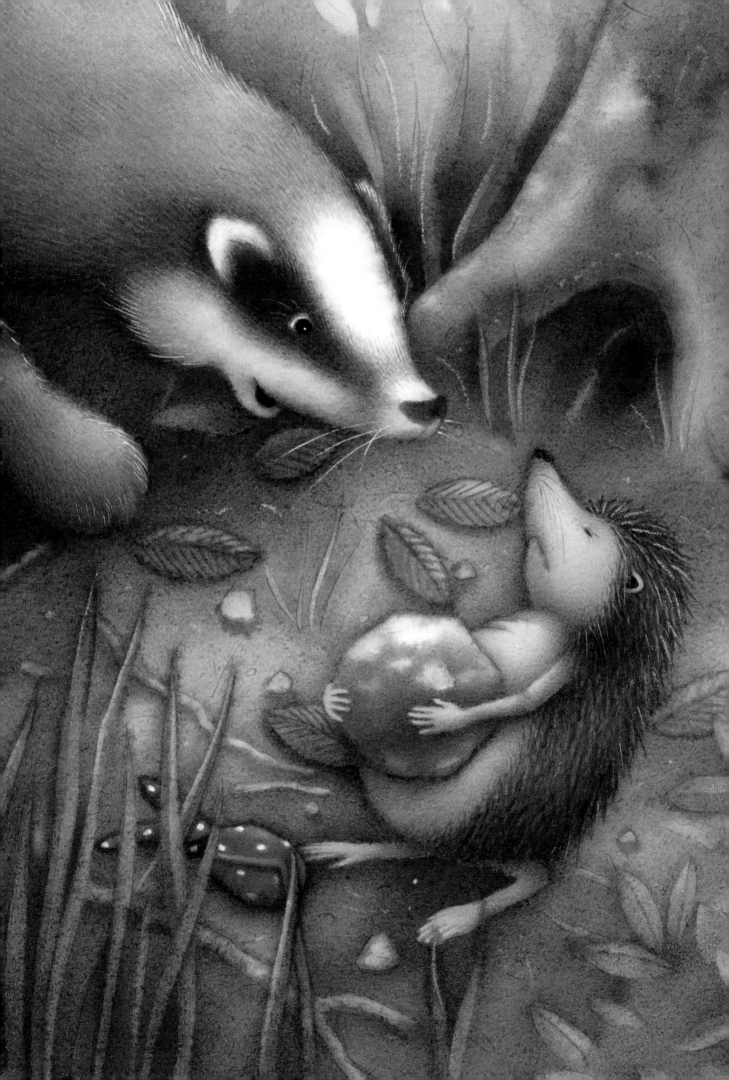

"Why would you want to be so strong?" asked Mikko.

"What do you mean, why? If I am the strongest in the world, then everyone will respect me. I wouldn't be afraid of anyone, and that would make me very happy."

Mikko thought this over. There were certainly advantages to being strong. "Could I give it a try?" he asked.

"Of course." Badger grinned. "Here, try first with a small stone."

Mikko grasped the stone and struggled to lift it up. He began to sweat. He got the stone up as far as his belly when it slipped to the ground and landed on his little toe.

"OUCH!" cried Mikko, rubbing the throbbing toe and whimpering. "This is silly!"

Mikko promised himself to only lift stones when he had to build a house or a wall around his herb garden. But just to get stronger? No thank you!

Mikko said good-bye to the badger and hobbled to the edge of the woods. There he saw a trail of ants. Fascinated, he watched the busy animals scurrying here and there. At first glance it seemed pointless, but when Mikko looked closer, he saw that each ant seemed to have a purpose and knew exactly where it was going.

"What are you doing?" he asked them. But the ants were so busy that they didn't even hear him.

His grandfather was right. All the animals were busy and ambitious. They wanted to become fast and smart and strong so they would be happy. But it seemed to Mikko that while they were striving, they weren't enjoying life at all.

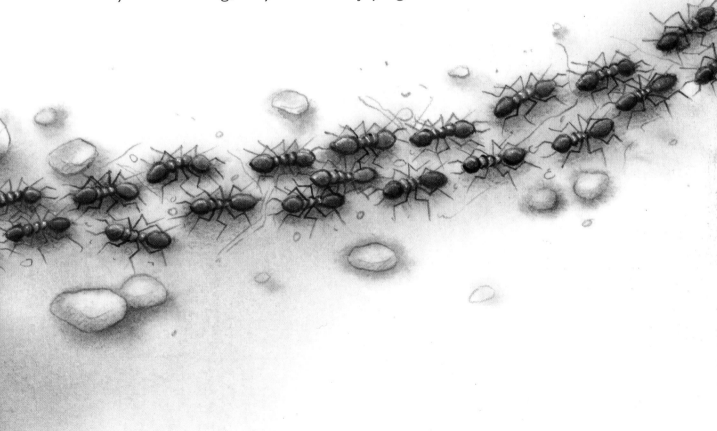

Did Mikko really want to live that way? Thoughtfully, he made his way home.

When he arrived back at his garden, with the singing birds, the beautiful plants, and the passing clouds, a wave of contentment washed over him.

No, I don't want to be the strongest, he thought, or the cleverest, or the fastest. Why make myself miserable just to be happy in the future when I'm already happy. I like the way I am now, here at home in my garden.

Mikko heard a hoarse cough and turned around. It was his grandfather.

"So, Mikko, did you go out and learn something today?"

"Yes, I did, Grandfather. But you're coughing. Sit down and I'll make you a cup of tea with herbs from my garden, mixed with fresh honey. That will certainly do you good."

"You think so?"

"Oh, yes! I know other healing herbs, too. I can help a sprained foot, a headache, and lots more."

"Is that so?" asked his grandfather.

Grandfather Tarek made himself comfortable among the herbs and flowers. He sipped his sweet tea, which did indeed help his cough. He asked Mikko questions. And with each answer, Grandfather Tarek saw how much his grandson really did know, and how much there was to learn in Mikko's garden.